MID
WAY
PRESS

Raw Deal is a work of fiction. All characters appearing in this work are a product of the author's imagination. Any resemblance to real persons, living or dead, is purely coincidental.

Published by Midway Press
A Division of Playfort Publishing
www.midwaypress.ca

Cover design by Otto Pfannschmidt
Printed and bound in Canada

Library and Archives Canada Cataloguing in Publication

Jackson, Melanie, 1956-
Raw deal / Melanie Jackson.

ISBN 978-0-9813164-5-1

I. Title.

PS8569.A265R38 2011 jC813'.6 C2011-906435-9

To my friend Chuck Currie

AFTER SHOT

Saturday, October 19, 10:02 a.m.

She aims the gun at my heart. "Go on, Colin. Jump."

We're on the Capilano Suspension Bridge. Far below, Capilano River swirls and foams over the jagged canyon rocks. I step sideways to glance down. The bridge sways. My guts twist.

Ray steps sideways, too. In her white-knuckle grip, the gun follows me like a homing device.

"You're going to jump," she says. "If you don't, I'll shoot you."

She can't mean it, not with those picnickers back there, in the park. She can't take the chance they'll look up. She's bluffing. She has to be.

I think of that rushing current, those sharp, pointy rocks.

"Forget it," I tell her.

Ray shrugs, and fires.

BEFORE SHOT

CHAPTER ONE

Friday, October 18, 12:05 p.m.

He claps an arm around my shoulders. His voice is easy, friendly. His eyes are laughing.

"C'mon, buddy. It'll be easy. You fill in for me, and I make it worth your while."

He's holding out two — no, three fifties.

I'm new to this school, but I already know who he is. Jace Turpin, of the Turpin's burger chain. Turpin's started here in North Vancouver, and new outlets are sprouting up all over British Columbia like grease bubbles on a grill. The Turpin's jingle, about its fat, juicy burgers, blitzes out of every local AM station: *sizzlin' and spicy!*

I can guess why Jace has zeroed in on me to sub for him as cashier/server at a nearby outlet. We're the same height. We have the same sandy hair and blue eyes.

Other kids are passing us in the hall. They stare at Jace. Several girls drool. He's the popular guy, the all-star, the charmer.

Jace turns his back on them. He murmurs, "At home, Dad has a security-camera feed into all our outlets. It's a black-and-white feed, though, and kind of hazy. He'll think you're me. See, every time I have a shift, Dad checks on me. That's the kind of controlling dude he is."

Poor little rich kid, I think. I start to pull away. I like the look of those fifties, but not of the deception they involve.

Jace doesn't let go of my shoulder. "Just this once. You get there at three a.m., open the joint. When your relief comes in at six, just turn and scram out the back. They'll think you're me. They won't question the behaviour of the boss's son."

He pulls two more fifties from his wallet. "Puh-leeze. I got a hot date, and I don't want to end it early. Know what I mean?" He flips his eyebrows up and down.

Sure I know. Don't we all have girls climbing over us at all hours?

Jace confides, "Dad's determined to make me work regular shifts like any other employee. He says it builds character."

"Yeah, well, I kind of have plans, too." I'm planning to install a new — well, new used — transmission in Mom's and my old Volvo. For a car buff, that's a hot date.

"Aw, c'mon, Colin. That's your name, right?"

"Yeah. Colin Wirt." I brace myself for the inevitable joke: *Wirt? Or maybe, Wart?*

That's the nickname I land with, no matter what school I go to. It started in kindergarten.

I had vague plans of smashing noses in. Then Mom pointed something out to me:

"Wart was the nickname they gave to King Arthur before he was crowned. The snobs looked down on him because he was just a servant. But it wasn't the snobs who pulled the sword from the stone. It was Wart."

Maybe it's hokey, but that story made me feel better. It calmed me down, at any rate, from plowing my stubby five-year-old fist into any schnozzes.

Jace surprises me. "Colin," he nods. "Well, Colin, this date I have Friday night. Rachel Manetas. Rachel's not just hot, she's ... "

He pauses, unable to come up with a comparison. He just gives me that charming grin.

I have a feeling Jace coasts on that grin quite a lot.

"She's sizzlin' like a Turpin's burger?" I fill in.

"Uh ... " Jace stares, puzzled. "Oh, I get it. Ha ha, funny guy. Good one."

He's pressing the fifties into my hand. "Be a sport, okay? Honestly, Colin. The plan is seamless. Help me out. I'll help you out."

He glances round. Right away, like a backup group, other kids passing by coo out greetings to him. I get the message. I'm new to the school. Jace as good as owns it. He'll smooth the way for me.

And I think: It'd be nice to have an in.

...

After Dad left us, Mom and I moved around a lot. Mom was working temp jobs while she went to university. Then she graduated and got a job in North Vancouver. So, we moved yet again.

With all this moving, I haven't had the chance to make a lot of friends. I haven't minded that much. I'm kind of a loner, I guess. I like to be self-reliant. To not have to depend on anyone, ever. Maybe it comes from trying to prove I don't need Dad, or maybe it's just natural to me. That's why I like to fix things myself. Not just our '88 Volvo, but household stuff that goes wonky. I can deal with it on my own.

This school, Grouse Mountain Secondary, is the first in a long time I'll be able to stay at for longer than a few months. Right to graduation, I'm hoping. And now Jace Turpin is offering me friendship, in exchange for a few hours dishing up burgers.

I realize I've closed my hand around the fifties. They give off that brand-new sound of crackling, like autumn leaves. I stare at their crisp red edges. I'm holding $250.

I have another thought. The used tranny I'm getting costs $190. I was going to charge it on the low-limit credit card Mom got me in case of emergency. I'd work the money off through a part-time job, hopefully in a garage.

With these fifties, anything I earn will be in the clear. I can pay cash for the tranny and not owe money on plastic.

Jace sees my frown, knows I'm wavering. His grin widens. He's confident I'll agree. Everything comes easy to someone like him.

CHAPTER TWO

I pull the Volvo into the Turpin's parking lot. This is the flagship outlet, the first one old man Turpin opened.

Of course, back then he was a young man. Son Jace was just a gleam in his eye.

A charming gleam, no doubt.

Switching off the engine, I suck back coffee from a thermos. The coffee's strong enough to launch an attack, but I need the jump-start to move my limbs from this seat.

I'm still bleary-eyed from installing the tranny. Around midnight, I crashed for a couple of hours. I wouldn't call what I had sleep, exactly. More like hallucinations of trannies.

Normal guys would dream about hot chicks like this Rachel Manetas, whoever she is.

One day, I'll be normal, too. One day, I'll get a life.

For tonight, I'm Jace's man, bought and paid for.

...

As I push it open, the Volvo door lets out a loud whine, which pretty well sums up my own feelings.

Except for the neon-red Turpin's sign, and a few house lights beyond some trees, I'm in darkness. Grouse Mountain, looming up behind Turpin's, is a giant inkblot blocking out the rest of the world. Its jagged peak swims in and out of view as charcoal clouds skid across the sky.

I start walking toward the Turpin's back door. In the red glow I see my breath preceding me in huge puffs.

I sling back the rest of the coffee. You signed on for this, Wirt. Now get through it.

I let myself in with the key Jace gave me. I blink. The joint is way too bright for the bleary-eyed. The darkness outside solidifies into unbroken black.

A gigantic silver grill stretches behind the serving counter. Its huge, closed lid can't keep the smell of cooking ground beef from escaping.

Jace explained the health-department-approved routine. *The staff closing up at midnight will have set an automatic timer. At 2:30 a.m., the patties start cooking on low. When you come in, lift the lid up, flip the burgers, and set the heat to medium-high. Even if a customer is waiting, cook the patties for ten minutes before you serve. It's important to cook the meat through, get it? Then turn the grill down to low again. The patties will keep till whenever.*

" 'The patties will keep till whenever,' " I mutter. Not a sentence likely to turn up in a Turpin's ad.

Along with other utensils, a long spatula hangs on the wall. Turning up the grill heat, I flip the patties.

Now, what else am I supposed to do? Oh, yeah. Put on a Turpin's apron and cap. *You gotta look the part, Colin old buddy.*

Because I'm playing a part, that's the whole point. A spare apron and cap hang beside the utensils. Pulling them on, I glance around for the security camera. There it is, aiming down from above the glass front door. If old man Turpin is watching, he'll think I'm Jace.

If old man Turpin is watching at this hour, he, too, needs to get a life.

I pull the cap down over my forehead. Jace said the film was grainy, but I suddenly feel self-conscious.

Let's see. My other duties include getting fries ready. They're frozen, in jumbo packages.

So much for the Turpin's ads about *fresh, fluffy fries!*

Out of customers' view, down a hall, there's a freezer. I stride toward it, past a plastic table and three chairs. I guess this is old man Turpin's idea of a staff room.

I hoist the freezer lid. It unsticks from the freezer with such a huge sigh that I almost don't hear the next sound —

A *creak!* from some metal lockers by the side door.

I pause, as cold air from the open freezer swirls up around me. "Anyone there?"

The hallway's quiet — but it's an uneasy kind of quiet, like somebody's holding their breath.

There's another sound, from out front this time. A pounding on the front door. It's so loud I can hear the glass rattle.

It's a pudgy guy, in jeans and a leather jacket cracking in several places. Unlocking the door, I let him in. Under the white light of the restaurant, I see he's middle-aged, with bloodshot eyes.

"I came by earlier and you weren't even open," he grumbles. "I thought the place was closed down. I got places to be, ya know?"

No, I don't know. "It's, like, five minutes to three," I point out.

"Yeah, yeah, you kids all have 'tude."

He shuffles to the counter and surveys the Turpin's menu.

Outside, the red neon of the Turpin's sign luridly outlines a truck with a huge, smiling cabbage painted on the side. A bubble extends out of its mouth: *Eat right with Hannah's Healthy Foods!*

If it were a civilized hour, I'd yuk at the irony of a healthy-foods truck driver breakfasting at Turpin's. Right now it only makes my mood worse.

While the guy's deciding, I dump the fries on a baking platter just about big enough to play field hockey on. I shove the platter in the oven and switch the dial to high. Then I empty a coffee packet and water into the coffee machine and press start.

"I could use summa that," the driver calls.

"Me, too. By prescription."

To my surprise, the guy chuckles. "All this time, I never realized you're a comedian."

All this time? I stare at him. Then I get it. He's a regular, and he thinks I'm the same kid who's always here early Saturday morning. He thinks I'm Jace.

I can just see Jace's winning smile: *See, Colin? It's a cinch.*

Yet for some reason I feel uneasy, like I just had a warning knock at the edge of my brain.

CHAPTER THREE

I figure if the truck driver can be good-humoured at this hour, so can I. I manage a friendly grin, then rustle up his order: a triple Turpin's burger layered with bacon, cheese, tomatoes, and onion. Plus, triple fries and triple-sized coffee.

Since the guy's into threes, I throw in three free packets of Turpin's chocolate chip cookies. If old man Turpin is watching on the security cam, he can deduct the cost from Jace's paycheck.

The driver crams his breakfast back with moans of pleasure. Then, slurping his coffee, he grabs a newspaper someone left on the next table. Pulling a pencil from his pocket, he licks the point to wet it, and starts in on Sudoku.

Nobody else is in sight, so I turn the grill down to low. I check on the fries. They're turning golden, if not exactly *fresh, fluffy!*

I refill the driver's coffee. He's shoved on a pair of glasses, the better to scowl through at Sudoku. Faulty eyesight: that would explain why he so easily mistakes me for Jace.

Again I feel that uneasiness, that vague alert to something wrong. I shrug it off. I don't make a habit of deceiving people, and this trick on old man Turpin is getting to me. That's all it is.

It's then I remember the whine from the end locker, and my sense that somebody was skulking around the back. At this point I pretty much chalk the idea up to early-morning heebie jeebies.

Still, it doesn't hurt to check.

I walk through the kitchen to the back hallway. I swing round the last locker. No one there. I try the locker doors. They all creak open, revealing uniforms, sweaters, beat-up running shoes.

No intruders.

Behind me, the door to the employee washroom is open a crack. I push it farther.

The window over the toilet is open, letting in cold air. It's a big enough window for someone slight, a girl maybe, to squeeze through.

But then I have something else to think about.

From the front, there's a violent sound of retching. The truck driver is throwing up, big-time.

...

He's still at it when I reach the front. He's heaving out the front door, which he's pushed wide. His face is red, swollen; his eyeballs bulge. With a loud gurgle in his throat, he tries to gulp back air — then heaves again.

Pinkish gobs are rolling down the door glass. The Turpin's welcome mat is a pool of barf.

Between upchucks, the driver fixes a terrified gaze on me. He can't control it.

I grab my cell phone from my back jeans pocket, ready to punch in 911.

The driver raises a hand so puffy it looks like a balloon. "No," he wheezes. Now that he's using his mouth to talk, the barf explodes out his nostrils. Along with it, he chokes out, "Can't miss this shift. Been in trouble lately for callin' in sick when I'm not. Gotta get this load delivered. Gotta meet some folks — "

I punch in 911 anyway. "Mister, look at yourself. You're barfing your guts out."

The guy shakes his head. He staggers over to his truck, leans against the driver's door, and barfs some more.

"North Vancouver Police Department, emergency," says a female voice in my ear.

"I'm at Turpin's on Capilano Road," I bark out as I run to the trucker. I consider tackling him, if necessary, to keep him here. As a vehicle operator he'd be a major road hazard.

He sees me coming, and climbs in the truck. He starts the engine. He's so out of it that he jams his foot down on the accelerator without shifting into drive. The engine revs into an ear-splitting roar. The guy sinks on to the wheel. Whether he's resting or fainted, I can't tell. The horn blares nonstop.

"I GOT A SICK MAN HERE," I yell into the phone. "LOOKS LIKE FOOD POISONING."

Over all the noise, I can't hear the dispatcher's reply. I'm betting she can't hear me, either.

In frustration I jump up on the running board and bang on the window. That rouses the driver, but not to listen to reason. Glaring at me, he shifts into drive. He floors the accelerator again.

The truck jumps forward, sending me flying. The phone slips from my hand. It crashes against the pavement and spins like a roulette wheel.

I get up, groaning. I've landed on my right elbow. I rub it. Blood comes off on my palm.

I stagger over to the phone, pick it up. "Hello?" I say.

Dead.

Great. I accepted Jace's money to get ahead of the debt game, and now I'll have to buy another cell phone.

I groan some more, this time inserting a few choice cuss words. I head back into Turpin's. Hopefully they have a Red Cross kit somewhere.

Behind me, footsteps squelch on the barf-saturated welcome mat.

I'm about to turn, when — *smash*. Something slams me in the skull.

CHAPTER FOUR

I reach for my phone, but it's doing the roulette-wheel thing again. The phone spins away from me. It morphs into the neon-red Turpin's sign. The sign whirls — then blinks off.

I come to. I'm in darkness. My head is killing me. So's my elbow. And the whole sorry package that is me is jolting around like — yeah, like a ball on a roulette wheel.

I'm curled around something. I push against it. It's rubbery, with grooves.

A tire.

I'm in a car trunk.

I'm lying on my right side. I stretch my left hand into the hollow of the tire and hold on. Then the jolting isn't so bad. I could easily go back to sleep.

It's warm in here, and getting warmer. I wouldn't mind some more sleep. Like for the next century or so ...

Faintly, through my mental fuzziness, a voice in my brain tells me to stay awake. It reminds me that carbon monoxide fumes could be creeping in.

Being bumped around will keep me conscious, I realize. I let go of the tire.

I think: Somebody knocked me out. They stuffed me in here. And now we're on a road with a lot of potholes.

Strains of music filter through the back wall of the trunk. I now know something else. Whoever this somebody is, they like country music.

It's a hot night in the country ... And it can only get hotter ...

A Tracy Byrd song. Tracy is right on. If more fumes are pouring into the trunk, it can only get hotter.

Killingly hot. And if the fumes don't get me, there's a good chance the person up front will. It's not like you kidnap people you're wishing a long, healthy life to.

Why would anyone kidnap me? What a joke.

A joke ...

The truck driver's face looms in my mind, pre-barf. He'd said:

All this time, I never realized you were a comedian.

Then, even in my fuzzified mental state, I get it.

The trucker mistook me for Jace Turpin — and so did the kidnapper.

...

I'm sweating, and not just because of the stuffy, hot air.

That Tracy Byrd fan up front is expecting a mega-payout from old man Turpin. He won't be pleased to find out he grabbed the wrong package.

With my left hand I grab the tire again. I hoist myself up. I twist around so that I'm facing the back of the car. Faintly, on either side, the rear lights glow.

I slide forward, my feet knocking against some objects that clank together. I reach back, feel for them. My fingers find cool, smooth sticks — skis. Another stick, with a metal U-shape at one end. A shovel.

And, a coil of rope.

As an everyday accessory to the car — or to tie me up with?

I press my palms against the inside of the trunk lid. I drag my fingers down till they meet a crack: the lid's bottom edge.

Below the crack, the carpet starts. The carpet's what I have to rip away. In newer cars than Mom's and my Volvo — which covers most of the cars on the planet — manufacturers install a cable on trunk floors. A yank on the cable disengages the lock. The trunk springs open.

It's a safety measure, for little kids who are playing around and are dumb enough to get trapped in the trunk.

…

Or, older kids who are dumb enough to sub for a millionaire's son.

I clench the edge of carpet and pull. But I can't get the carpet loose.

From the front I hear Tracy Byrd crooning. His problem is women. Mine's survival.

The thought chills me. The chill tightens my muscles. I dig my fingers into the carpet again.

At the same moment, the car takes a hairpin turn. To avoid being thrown backward, I grip the edge of carpet even harder.

With the force of my grip, the carpet wrenches loose.

...

I scrabble around under the carpet till I feel the cable. I yank on it.

Nothing.

Wriggling on to my side, I bring my feet up. I push my soles against the bottom part of the trunk lid. I pull the cable and don't let go. The effort is killing me, but I don't let go.

There's a clean *pop!*, like the sound of a tennis ball hitting the centre of a racquet. The trunk lid bounces open.

...

I push the lid higher — but not too high, in case the driver sees it in his rearview mirror. Just enough for me to sit up and lean out, gasping in the fresh air.

We're on a dirt road, surrounded by forest. Grouse's peak, muddied by the floating clouds, looms closer than it did from Turpin's. I'm guessing we're on an old logging road.

The car — I think it's a Mustang GT — keeps climbing. Far below, like a jumble of silver coins, stretch the lights of Vancouver across the Burrard Inlet.

The Mustang's right rear wheel plunges into a deep, wide pothole. The tire spins.

The car's stuck.

If the driver keeps spinning the wheel, like most people will do for a while out of sheer frustration, I have a chance to jump out. To run.

But the driver door opens. With a curse, the driver gets out. His footsteps crunch on stones and twigs.

He's heading round to the back of the car.

…

He wants the shovel. He's going to move dirt under the tire to give it some traction.

I lower the trunk lid almost shut. I don't want the kidnapper to know I've released the lock.

The crunching stops in front of me. He's hesitating. He doesn't know what condition I'm in: still unconscious or slightly awake and groggy. He didn't think he'd have to open the trunk just yet.

Still holding the lid shut, I shift so that I'm lying on my back. I draw my knees to my chest.

I hear the clank of keys. He's going to open the trunk.

So he thinks.

Letting go of the lid, I smash my feet straight up against it.

Thunk! It smashes into the guy's face, knocking him backward.

I scramble out. My kidnapper struggles to a sitting position. Blood's pouring from his nose. Stunned, he's shaking his head to try to clear it.

In the rear lights I see his face.

It's Jace Turpin.

CHAPTER FIVE

I see something else. Jace has a gun in one hand.

I grind my foot on his wrist. He drops the gun. I pick the gun up and hurl it into the dark. I keep my foot on his wrist. "Little rich boys shouldn't play with guns," I tell him.

Then I stand away. Jace staggers to his feet. His mouth is hanging open: he's in shock. Something's gone wrong, and that just doesn't happen to Jace Turpin.

He squints vainly up the dark road. "That was Ray's gun," he mumbles. "She bought it from a guy on the Downtown Eastside. She'll be pissed."

Ray?

Well, Colin, this date I have Friday night. Rachel Manetas.

Rachel — Ray — who's so hot she sizzles like a Turpin's burger.

In his other hand, Jace still holds the 'stang keys. He adjusts them so one of each is sticking out between his fingers. The old self-defence routine.

I pre-empt the gouges he was planning for my face. I swing my right fist out, slamming him in the jaw. He falls. I jump on top of him. I raise my fist for a possible return engagement with his nose, which is still spouting blood.

I warn, "You tell me what this is about, or I'll wipe your nose for you — right off your face."

My weight is making it hard for Jace to breathe. "Okay," he gasps. "Okay, I'll talk. We were gonna let you go." He's trying to smile. To win me over, like he always wins people over. "It's just a, a trick on my old man. We pretend I've been kidnapped. He pays out some dough; we get a windfall."

I think of the fifties Jace brandished at me. When I'd hesitated about trading places with him, he'd produced yet more. There seemed to be no end of them.

"You have enough dough," I say in disbelief. "A fake kidnapping? What're you doing something so stupid for?"

"For fun," Jace replies, surprised, as if he's explaining to a none-too-bright little kid. "For something to do. And, to get back at Dad for hassling me all the time. For finding fault with me, 24/7."

I remember what Jace said earlier, about the security camera. *Every time I have a shift, Dad checks on me. That's the kind of controlling dude he is.*

Jace sees I'm thinking. He tries wriggling free.

I grab a hank of his hair, forcing his head way back. "I'm not finished with you, buddy. I want answers. How were you going to do it?"

His eyes water at the pain. "We already sent Dad a cellphone photo of me tied up. We texted him not to call the police, or I'd be killed. Next, we were gonna text Dad ransom instructions. He'd have to make a drop — a hundred grand, in cash — up the road, in an old cabin. After that, I'd rough myself up and go home. Pretend I'd escaped the kidnappers."

In the light from the open driver's door, I notice a jagged gash on the right side of Jace's temple. Looks like a glass cut. This must be the roughing up. I have to hand it to him. It looks pretty convincing.

"And me?" I demand. "What was my role in all this?"

Tears are spilling down Jace's cheeks. He's suffering too much to lie. "We were gonna leave you in the cabin, knocked unconscious. I'd claim you and another guy kidnapped me. You'd take the fall."

Rage rises, like bile, up through my chest and into my brain. I want so badly to punch the rest of Jace's face in. But I know if I start punching him, I'll keep going till he's pulp.

Jace pleads, "We'll go for a different plan, Colin. We'll cut you in. It'll be a good deal for you. Ray's waiting for us, up the road, at the cabin. You come with me, as a partner, not a prisoner. I promise, Colin. I'll square it with Ray. Please."

He's dripping tears like a wet mop. Disgusted, I let him go. The cops can deal with him.

...

I wrench the car keys from Jace. He's too busy holding on to his head and moaning to notice or care.

I stagger over to the trunk. Removing the shovel, I start filling the pothole in with dirt. It's easy, because it rained last night and the dirt is damp. Then I toss the shovel back in the trunk, where it clatters against the skis. Two pairs of them, I notice in the trunk's dim light. One pair is hot-pink, with the initials R.M.

Rachel Manetas.

Rachel and Jake. Just another wholesome couple enjoying the outdoors together.

I slam the lid shut and head to the driver's door.

Jace tries to get up, but he's in too much pain. He sways and falls back.

He snivels, "Wait, don't leave me here. Hey, Colin, c'mon. I meant it about cutting you in on the deal."

I swing into the driver's seat and shut the door. I call back, "Forget it, buddy. Any deal of yours is a raw deal for me."

Starting the engine, I press the accelerator down slowly. The car eases forward.

I've caught a break. Dawn is starting. Grey is trickling over Grouse Mountain. I can see to avoid any more mammoth potholes.

As I drive off, I see Jace's astonished face in the rear lights. He can't believe I passed on his deal. He can't believe things aren't turning out the way he, Jace Turpin, wants them to. His jaw is hanging down in a slack, stunned O.

…

I slam my palm against the wheel, in anger at Jace for playing me, in frustration at myself for going along.

And, in disappointment about school. From now till grad day I'll be the outsider who reported Jace to the cops. I know how it works. It doesn't matter that Jace is one-hundred-proof guilty of assault. Of attempted fraud against his own dad. It won't make any difference. I'll be the bad guy for squealing on him. I'll be on my own, as always.

Well, I'm used to that. I can live with it.

I'm sure Jace expects me to forget the whole thing. Even now his winning smile spreads from one edge of my brain to the other in widescreen persuasion. *C'mon, Colin. Help me out. I'll help you out.*

I slam my palm against the wheel again. "Yeah," I say out loud. "And then, one day, you'll torpedo some other schmuck with one of your con games."

Having made the decision, I calm down. I plan my moves. First, I'll get my own car back from the Turpin's lot. I'll go home and soak my head in an extra long, extra hot shower. Then, I'll go to the cops.

Wait. The lessons of a thousand *CSI*s come back to me. Better to visit the cops right off. Let them see my head wound just as it is. Let them take fingerprints off me. I'm wearing Jace's prints all over.

The fir trees are thinning. The old road curves round to join a dead-end neighbourhood street. The car gives one parting lurch, and then we're on pavement.

...

It'll be long time before I get to muscle a highway again in a GT. I might as well enjoy the ride back to Turpin's. I cruise the Mustang along, enjoying its smoothness. At a feather touch, it purrs into high speed, where the old Volvo would clank and resist.

By now the dawn is spilling pink and orange over the mountainside. Pulling over to the shoulder, I let the top down. I sit for a while. On my injured head, the cool air is sweet, healing.

I don't know how many minutes I stay there. But after a while a car zooms past me, about double the speed limit.

It breaks the spell. I start the motor again. I take the road slowly this time. I'll have to face the real world soon enough.

...

I pull up to the Turpin's lot, but I can't drive into it. Strung from posts, yellow police tape cordons off the lot. Cop cars, their top lights glowing and spinning, surround the restaurant. With the lights and the Turpin's neon sign, the lot is soaked in red light.

I see plainclothes detectives milling around inside the restaurant. Outside, uniformed cops are standing guard along the tape.

I think: Somebody saw me being assaulted and kidnapped. Maybe it was the truck driver. Yeah, that could be it. Realizing he was too sick to drive, the guy stopped across the road. He reported what he saw, and now the cops are looking for clues.

Well, I'm about to cut down on their workload.

I park the Mustang by the sidewalk, past a bus-stopping area. I start toward the nearest cop, who's standing, arms folded and grim-faced, by the yellow tape.

Before I get to the cop, a freckle-faced girl, kind of plain, walks up to him from inside the taped-off area. She looks pale, scared. So scared that she forgot to remove her Turpin's apron and cap before leaving.

She's the six a.m. relief, I realize.

I can't hear what the girl says, but the cop nods at her. She walks out of the lot. She heads down the sidewalk, towards me.

Closer, I notice how her freckles stand out like sand particles against her pale skin. I see that she has large, hazel eyes that make her not so plain, after all.

I want to tell her that she doesn't have to be scared. That the kidnapping she heard about is over.

I stop, unsure whether to say anything. I should go straight over to the police.

Through tear-blurred eyes, the girl sees me. "Oh my God … Jace?"

Wiping the back of her hand over her wet eyes, she stares hard at me. "I'm, I'm sorry," she gulps. "Just for a second there, I thought I'd — sorry, it's stupid. I thought you were a ghost."

The word *ghost* drains the air out of my chest. Grabbing her wrist, I croak, "What do you mean?"

The girl bites her lower lip to steady it. "S-somebody shot Jace, up an old logging road on Grouse Mountain. Jace phoned for help, but by the time they got there, it was too late. He was dead."

CHAPTER SIX

"No," I protest. A nightmare is spreading around me, a black hole waiting to suck me in. "No. I just left Jace up there. He's ... "

The girl's hazel eyes gape, frightened. She glances back at the cop.

"Don't say anything," I say. I drag her along the sidewalk, past a tall fir tree. Its wide, needle-thick base is like a skirt, shielding us.

She's too surprised to resist. But that won't last long. Already she's pulled free. "You're the one they're looking for. I overheard them. You're Colin Wirt."

A cop car drives past. The cop at the wheel glances at us.

The girl heaves a big breath, preparing for a mega scream.

I reach for the girl, pull her tight against me. I press my mouth against her ear. "Don't give me away," I whisper. "Please. I didn't know Jace was dead. His murder is the worst thing that could happen to me."

I close my eyes, vainly trying to block the images my brain is throwing back at me. My tussle with Jace. My prints on him. Probably my blood. All the *CSI*-type stuff I thought would back my story up — it's going to condemn me. The police will think I killed Jace.

The cop turns away. I spot a slight grin. She thinks we're boyfriend-girlfriend, lovin' it up. She swings her car into the Turpin's lot.

I release the girl. "I'm sorry," I say. "I had no right to grab you like that. I'm pretty messed up."

The girl's wide, hazel eyes study me, trying to figure me out. She's giving me a chance.

"You need to sit down," she says finally. "You need to relax. You can tell me what happened."

I peer round the fir tree into the Turpin's lot. There's Mom's and my Volvo. The door's open. A cop's sitting there, taking notes. He will have checked the insurance papers, phoned Mom by now. That's why they're looking for me.

I feel in my pocket. My hand closes on Jace's car keys. "I'll give you a lift home," I offer. "And yeah, I'd like to tell you about what happened. Talking about it will help me."

She hesitates. "It's okay. I live close by."

"Yeah, I know," I say. "Your mother warned you never to accept a ride with murder suspects. I understand. And — thanks for not screaming just now."

I'm about to turn away. I pause. "Hey, tell me your name. You're the only nice thing that's happened to me in all this."

Her freckled face spreads into a shy smile. “Bex Yarrow,” she says.

I smile back. “Hi Bex.”

I walk toward the Mustang. I’m almost there when I hear sudden, running footsteps behind me.

Bex catches up. “Sure, I’ll take a lift — Colin.”

...

I pull the Mustang into the school parking lot, under a low-hanging maple. Its leaves are orange, red, yellow. As I tell her my story, the leaves fall slowly, gracefully, onto the hood.

“So Ray’s the only other person who knows the truth,” I finish. “Who can back up my story.”

“What about this truck driver, the one who got sick?” Bex demands. “Maybe he saw something.”

I shrug. “In his condition, he’s probably mowed the Hannah’s Healthy Foods truck into a lamppost by now. Besides, he thought I was Jace. He didn’t know I was just subbing for him.”

Bex exhales a frustrated sigh. Settling back in her seat, she stares out. Under the low branches we can see the school’s basement windows.

She sees me following her gaze, and grins. “That’s my home away from home,” she explains. “The old part of the school library. A few of us hang out there. The moles, they call us, because it’s so dark and dingy.”

She smiles that shy smile again. “If you’re ever looking for me, that’s where I’ll be, Colin.”

I like the way Bex says my name. Not as if she believes me to be a murder suspect. As if she believes in me.

"I'd look for you in a second," I tell her, meaning it, and Bex blushes.

I remember how she was crying when I first saw her, outside Turpin's. "You must've liked Jace."

"Oh, sure. Everyone liked Jace. Especially Rachel Manetas. Ray's new to Grouse, like you. You should've seen Ray double-take when Jace walked by. She was into him, and bad. Everyone noticed, even the out-of-it kids like me."

A sunny yellow leaf flutters on to the hood.

Into him, and bad.

Well, maybe. But I'm guessing the botched kidnap plan changed Ray's feelings.

Enough for her to kill Jace?

CHAPTER SEVEN

I think hard. I threw the gun away from Jace. But dawn was up when I drove away. He could've found the gun, then headed to the cabin where Ray was waiting. Furious at Jace for bungling their plan, she grabbed the gun and —

I grip the steering wheel. I'm picturing an orange flash of gunfire against the grey morning air.

"What are you thinking about, Colin?"

"I have to confront Ray."

Bex wrinkles up her nose, melding the freckles. "Shouldn't you let the police do that?"

"Yeah, but by then she'll have a story together. It could be me they assign to make licence plates."

Then I ask abruptly, "Would it be okay if I looked up Rachel's address at your place? I need to get to her while she's still freaked. Unless she's totally inhuman, she'll give something away."

Bex shakes her head. "You're nuts, taking on a possible murderer by yourself. But sure. We can look up Ray's address. We'll have to be quiet, though. Saturday mornings my mother likes to catch up on her beauty sleep."

...

We leave the Mustang under the maple tree. I don't dare use the 'stang anymore. I'm guessing that, about now, Jace's car is number two on the police's search list. Right after me.

We don't see anyone as we walk, except a kid tossing newspapers onto door stoops from his bike. He doesn't look at us. He's busy listening to his iPod.

Bex's house is a faded grey clapboard, with small windows. Firs tower over it.

She unlocks a side door. We're in the kitchen; a narrow stairway leads down to the basement. "There's a computer down there, and a phone," she whispers.

The ceiling rumbles. Bex glances up nervously. It rumbles again. I realize it's her mother, snoring.

Bex whispers, "Mother's kind of strict. If she finds a boy here, at this hour ... "

She's pale again, the freckles sticking out. This time they make me think, not of sand, but of dozens of warning signs. She's taking a risk for me.

"I won't be long," I promise. "I appreciate this."

Her jitters have infected me. I glance at the ceiling, too. "May Mother's Zs continue," I whisper, and Bex relaxes into a smile. A faint one.

…

There's a door at the bottom of the basement steps. I shut it behind me, head over to the phone, and punch in my home number.

"Mom?"

"Colin! Where are you? What's going on? The police want to see you about a murder. It's all over the TV."

I hear the murmur of our TV in the background.

"I didn't do it, Mom. Jace Turpin and his girlfriend kidnapped me. It was a con scheme to get ransom from his dad."

While talking, I've grabbed a phone book. I flip through to the M's. Mah, Mahler, Maldor, Mamet …

Manetas. 148 Panorama Ridge Road.

"The police will believe you, Colin. You're an honest boy. Tell me where you are, and I'll come and get you. We'll go to the police station together."

I search for a patch of sleeve that's blood-free and wipe it across my forehead. Mom's so sure of what's right. So sure everyone else will see it as clearly as she does.

But getting the cops to believe me would be about as easy as pulling a real-life sword from a stone.

"I'm at Bex Yarrow's house," I say wearily. "Bex is a girl from school — she works the six a.m. shift at Turpin's. Or was going to, till it became a crime scene.

"But don't come here," I add quickly. "I don't want to get Bex in trouble with her mom."

Mom's voice interrupts with sudden, sharp urgency. "Are you near a TV? Turn it on right away. The CBC all-news network."

There's a TV on a table by the wall, above a DVD player and next to an ironing board and a basket of clothes. Turning on the TV, I see that DVDs with weepy titles are piled on top: *Love Story, Terms of Endearment, Message in a Bottle*. Each DVD bears a strip of masking tape, with large, black letters magic-markered on: PROPERTY OF MRS. FLORA LOUISE YARROW.

On one DVD, Mrs. Yarrow pressed the magic marker so hard she cracked the plastic case.

Strict? Mrs. Yarrow is downright weird.

The Yarrows' TV is old. It's taking a minute to blink on. I look around the room some more, this time at photos on the wall. Amid some moody black-and-white North Van landscapes, there's a shot of Bex with a big, pasty woman. I can make out a resemblance — just.

With a smile that's more of a snarl, Mrs. Yarrow has her arm clamped around Bex's shoulders. In a hug or an oxygen-depriving squeeze, it's hard to tell.

The TV flickers on at last. It's a Saturday morning 'toon. In a jumpy image, Scooby Doo and friends are chowing down on burgers.

Not a pleasant association for me right about now. I punch in the all-news network channel.

An anchorwoman is speaking:

" ... and we see Jace Turpin, early this morning, on the Turpin's security-camera tape."

A grainy black-and-white video pops up. Today's date shows at the bottom, along with the time: 3:21 a.m. And the location: Turpin's Grouse Mountain outlet.

A blond kid stands with his back to the camera. He's flipping burger patties. That's me, I think. And there's the truck driver, playing Sudoku as he waits for his triple-helping breakfast.

"The kid's me, not Jace," I tell Mom. "And the customer's a Hannah's Healthy Foods trucker who later erupted in a major barf fest."

Mom doesn't say anything. We keep watching, mesmerized by the grainy tape.

The Yarrows' TV flickers. Maybe it's not the TV. Maybe the cable connection is wonky.

Now the image is clear again. The blond kid at the grill sets down his spatula. He turns. He strolls around the service counter, and right up to the camera.

He rolls his eyes around, sticks out his tongue, and grins.

"No," Mom whispers at the other end of the line.

Because I was wrong. It's not me, after all.

It's Jace.

CHAPTER EIGHT

The CBC freezes the security-camera frame on Jace's grin. The anchorwoman comments in a voiceover:

"So, we know young Jace was safe as of 3:21 a.m. Twenty minutes later, according to police, a gloved hand reached up to smash the camera with a rock. Sadly, this ?lm of Jace Turpin is the last that his dad, the owner and founder of Turpin's restaurants, will ever have of him."

New image. Mom's and my old Volvo, saturated in the red neon light of the Turpin's sign. The anchorwoman continues, "Police aren't revealing how Jace was killed. They'll only say that they're looking for the driver of this vehicle, one Colin Wirt. They say that Wart — "

The anchorwoman gives a cute, embarrassed smile. "Looks like I need my morning coffee! Sorry, folks. Police will only say that Wirt is a person of interest."

Next up onscreen: my grad photo, taken last week for the Grouse Mountain Secondary yearbook.

I'm sick, dizzy. That big black hole seeps close to my feet again. I'm about to fall in.

Mom's been quiet up to now, watching the TV. "Colin," she says. Her worried but calm tone pulls me back from the hole, back to consciousness. "There has to be an explanation. Were you away from the front of the restaurant at 3:21 a.m.? Could Jace have slipped into Turpin's without your knowing?"

I go over and switch off the TV. I'm trying to remember 3:21 a.m. "After I served the Hannah's guy, I went to the back. I wanted to check out a noise I'd heard. That could've been around then.

"Yeah, Jace could've come in. He could've slipped around the edge of the restaurant without the camera catching him. It's trained on the service counter. This was Jace's chance to jam his face up into the camera. It'd be handy later," I note bitterly, "when I tried to give the cops my version of events."

Mom starts to speak, but I'm remembering something else. The cold breeze that hit me while I was checking out the back. The open washroom window. Someone was hiding in the back, and beat it out before I saw them.

Them? More likely, her. Ray.

But why was Ray inside Turpin's? Still holding the phone, I sink on to the Yarrows' faded check sofa and knead my forehead.

"The trucker is our answer," Mom says. "Jace came in while you were at the back. The trucker would have noticed him open the door."

"I dunno. The trucker was pretty involved with his Sudoku."

"We'll tell the police about the trucker, Colin. They'll ?nd him."

...

There's a creak. The basement doorknob twists.

I jump up, expecting Mrs. Flora Louise Yarrow to barge in. She's heard something. She thinks I'm a burglar, after her DVD collection.

The door opens. I gape stupidly, wondering what possible explanation I can give for being here. *Honest, Mrs. Yarrow, I'm not into weepers.*

But it isn't Mrs. Yarrow. It's Bex, with a BLT sandwich that smells so good I feel weak.

"Hey, thanks. I didn't realize how hungry I was." I hold up the phone. "I'm just talking to my mom."

Bex brightens. "Oh, good. She must've been so worried. Have you ?gured anything out?"

I shake my head. "If anything, I'm more stumped than before."

What was the point of Ray hiding in the back? Jace had to have a key to the side door. He and Ray could've let themselves in whenever they felt like it. They could've waited till the trucker left, then come in and clobbered me.

They had no way of knowing I'd fall off the Hannah's truck and be easier prey than they'd expected.

Something doesn't ?t. I can sense it, but I can't see it.

All at once, from outside, sirens pierce the basement.

Bex's hazel eyes are enormous. She whispers, "The police."

...

My mother's voice apologizes over the line. "It's for the best, Colin. You can't ?gure this out on your own. The police will listen. They will hear you out."

Those minutes when Mom wasn't saying anything. When I thought she was silently watching the TV. She'd gone to get her cell. She'd phoned the cops on me.

Footsteps stomp overhead. A yell blasts out. "Bex? Why are the cops outside?"

I click the phone off, set it down. I wheel around.

The basement is only half-underground. Sliding windows look out on to the backyard. I open one and climb through.

Mrs. Yarrow is stomping down the stairs. Any moment now she'll be through that door.

I'm about to make a break for it when there's a tug on my sleeve.

It's Bex, holding out the sandwich. "Here," she whispers. "You'll need this."

I take it gratefully. "You're a brave kid," I whisper back. "I'll get through this, and I'll come back to see you, okay?"

She nods. I hightail it for the forsythia bushes at the back of the yard. Their yellow petals glow garishly in the still-grey early morning.

I plow through the forsythias into the neighbours' yard.

I hear the police banging on the Yarrows' door, shouting at them to open up. I hear Mrs. Yarrow's hoarse, accusing yells from the basement.

I hear the loud smack she lands on Bex.

CHAPTER NINE

No wonder Bex is so timid. No wonder she's a "mole" at school, hiding with the other shy kids in the basement when not in class. With a mom like Flora Louise, it's amazing Bex even has the confidence to step outside her front door.

Cramming back the BLT sandwich, I jog through backyards. The streets aren't safe for me. I've already glimpsed one police cruiser rolling by.

It's just after seven, so I'm hoping people are still enjoying their Saturday sleep-in.

I head north. I have to find Panorama Ridge. Specifically, 148 Panorama Ridge.

Because Ray and I have a rendezvous with the truth.

I'm going on the theory that, with a name like Panorama, Ray's street is as high up the mountain as the 'hood extends.

The 'hood is called Grouse Woods, because it's clustered around the base of the mountain. Everything is pretty close.

It occurs to me that I should clean up before I confront Ray. She's more likely to talk to me if I look human, as opposed to a war casualty.

Gulping down the last of the BLT, I swerve to the side of a house. I want a hot, hour-long shower, but right now I'll settle for a few minutes under an outdoor tap. Finding one, I turn it on full-blast. I remove my sweatjacket and T, then douse my head in the onrush of icy water, scrubbing to get rid of the dried blood. I only wish I could scrub the past few hours away, too.

I notice that, in the next yard, sheets and pillowcases are strung on a clothesline. Probably someone forgot to pull them down last night. I sprint over and use one of the sheets to dry off. It's damp with dew, but the sun is higher now. I feel some warming rays.

"Git!"

Whoops. Just my luck to attract an early bird. Raising my hands in surrender, I back away.

A lean, wiry old woman is wagging a bony forefinger over a second-storey windowsill. "Just when I thought my linens were all done, all nice and clean — you've spoiled them!"

Embarrassed about being caught half-dressed, I pull my T and sweatjacket back on. I edge toward the fence separating the old woman's yard from her neighbours'. "Uhhh ... let's look on the bright side. I didn't go near the pillowcases."

Her scowl intensifies. "You're a hoodlum, that's what you are. I time the drying of my linens. I allow for the freshness of morning dew."

Then, abruptly, the old woman's voice softens. Becomes friendly, in a whiny kind of way. "Why, it's Jace Turpin."

Obviously she hasn't switched on her morning news. I hesitate. If I can pass for Jace, maybe she'll forget about this incident.

She's beaming down at me. "Jace Turpin, you always were one for mischief!"

I put my hand over my eyes, pretending to shield them from the sun. I'm actually shielding my face from her view.

Remembering Jace's winning smile, I put on one of my own. "Ma'am, my brain isn't working this morning. Can you tell me where Panorama Ridge is?"

She wags a finger. "You're foolin' with me. Hold it. I bet you've been drinking, haven't you, young Jace?"

I can't keep up this inane smile. My facial muscles are starting to ache.

The woman isn't beaming anymore. She's squinting at me. "Panorama Ridge is two streets up. But you should know that."

"I do now," I reply. I run to the fence, and climb over into the next yard.

Where a fluffy white poodle rushes at me, barking.

...

I make it back over the fence on to the old woman's property, but not before the poodle closes its teeth on my right ankle. *Chomp.* I kick the dog off. Whimpering, it falls back.

It's a toss-up whether I should seek out Ray or go to the ER for a tetanus shot.

Ray wins out. Old habits die hard. I have to figure out this problem, my way, on my own. I have to fix it.

I decide to give up trespassing through back yards, though. Thanks to the poodle, I'm now sporting a limp. I can't shuttle over any more fences.

Reaching Panorama Ridge, I hobble along to 148.

...

My plan isn't brilliant or original. It's to knock on the door and ask to see Ray.

On the circular driveway I walk past a sleek green Mercedes and up to the panelled front door. I have knuckles raised, ready to knock, when I hear music coming from round the side of the house.

It's a hot night in the country

Taking us to an all-time high ...

I flash back to the Mustang's steaming hot, oxygen-challenged trunk. To the strains of Tracy Byrd filtering from the front, where Jace Turpin was listening to it.

I abandon the straightforward approach. Except for the music, there's no sign of life in the house. I head around the side.

I find a terrace with a wide-angle view of Vancouver, clear from Lions Gate Bridge in the west to Second Narrows Bridge in the east. I don't know if my brain can compute real-estate value this high.

And Ray and Jace were into a kidnap scheme for something to do.

One of the glass doors to the terrace is propped open with a purse, to let in the fresh morning air. Inside, a girl is jogging on a treadmill to Tracy Byrd.

Singing along with him, she doesn't notice me. I lean on the edge of the door and stare at her.

She's tall and slim, with almond-shaped green eyes and long, straight reddish-brown hair. She doesn't pace on the treadmill so much as slink on it, like a cat. Her face is heart-shaped, with a bit of a pointed chin. This gives her a sly look. Again I think of a cat.

Yeah, I can see why Jace found Ray Manetas sizzlin' hot.

Pausing like I'm doing is a bad idea. It makes me realize how tired I am. I'd like to slump down in one of the terrace's lawn chairs. To snooze to the sound of Tracy Byrd, and this girl singing along with him.

But sleep isn't a luxury murder suspects can indulge in.

Shoving my hands into my pockets, I walk inside. "I see you're playing our song."

CHAPTER TEN

Ray's so startled she trips forward on the treadmill. I reach out to catch her arm, preventing her from falling.

I say, "Yeah, it's me, Colin Wirt. The guy you and Jace were going to frame."

Ray's green eyes blaze. Jumping off the treadmill, she whips a towel off the nearby sofa. At first I think she's going to slap me with it. Instead, she wraps it around her neck and glares.

"How dare you trespass into my house," she hisses. "The police are after you. I saw it on the news early this morning. I heard you were dangerous. They should have added, *loony*. Now take your crazy babbling and get out."

Ray sure has the imperious routine down. I guess she's like Jace, used to everything going her way. These rich kids.

It occurs to me that the nickname Ray doesn't suit her. It's too casual, too inadequate. She should stick to Rachel. Or maybe, given that off-with-his-head glare, Queen Rachel.

I sink on to the white, plush leather sofa. The whole room is white. Kind of blinding when you've been bashed on the head. I look straight back at Ray, unflinching before those narrowed green eyes. "You've had your fun, your something-to-do, and now Jace is dead. Why not go to the cops before they come to you?"

I put more confidence into my voice than I feel. But I'm rewarded with a sudden spark of fear in those almond-shaped greens. In a hard voice, Ray says, "They can't prove anything. No one can."

"You killed Jace Turpin, didn't you?"

That fear springs into her eyes again, sharper than before. She swings her hand back, ready to slap me.

Then she clenches her hand, stopping its momentum.

And bursts into tears. "I didn't mean to. Honestly."

Being vulnerable, she's more appealing. And more dangerous.

I stand up, half-despising the sobbing Ray, half-wanting to comfort her. I settle my conflicted feelings by grabbing a box of tissues off a coffee table. I shove it at her.

She pulls out a whole bunch of tissues and wipes at her eyes. "Who are you, to be hurling accusations at people? *You* look like you just stepped out of a car crash. No — you look like you ARE a car crash." She honks her nose into the tissues.

"Save the insults for later, Ray. When you've confessed to the police and have started serving your time. I'll come and visit you in jail, and you can insult me for hours on end, if you want."

She scowls at me, eyes bright with fresh tears. "It's Rachel to you. And I'm not going anywhere near jail."

Her mouth stops trembling. A sly smile crooks at it. "I'd scram if I were you. All I have to do is start screaming. My dad will hear, and rush down. Know what? He's a judge, Colin. Very influential — and very hot-tempered. He'll think you're forcing yourself on me. You'll be toast."

"Save your threats," I say shortly. "No one would believe you. You're not my type, anyway."

Like heck she isn't, with those almond-shaped green eyes and that mocking set to her mouth. And that slinky way of moving. Geez. Even when honking her nose, she's slinky.

She shrugs. "No? Not that I'm interested, but what is your type, then, Colin Wirt?"

Unbidden, Bex Yarrow comes into my mind. Shy Bex, with the mean mother and the golden heart. Ballsy Bex, pressing a sandwich on me when the cops were about to swarm her house. Bex should be any guy's type.

I lean toward Ray, so that she instinctively backs away. "Your dad, the big-wheel judge, isn't the only one around here who's hot-tempered. Is he, Ray? That's why you killed Jace. You couldn't control your rage at him for bungling — ”

“NOOOO!” she screams, clapping her hands to her ears.

Rerun time. Expecting angry parental footsteps, I raise my eyes to the ceiling.

Luckily Judge Manetas is a deep sleeper. There’s just silence.

I lower my gaze to Ray. Having depleted her oxygen supply, she’s gulping raggedly, angrily, for breath.

“Planning on an encore?” I inquire.

“Just. Get. Out.”

That seems to be all anyone ever says to me anymore.

It’s not a dignified exit. I walk right into the glass door. At some point Ray’s purse fell over, so the door slid shut.

I don’t glance back as I open it and exit. I know that mocking gaze will be back, and I can’t take it.

...

I’ve confronted Ray, and she’s admitted killing Jace. Now the police can deal with her. They’re the professionals. They’ll question her without being distracted by green eyes and a cat-like smile.

I can turn myself in now. Unless a cop car spots me, I’ll go home and phone the police from there. That way, Mom will be with me when they come. She’d like that.

I'll tell you a story, Colin. Long ago, there was a boy named Wart. He pulled a sword from a stone.

Yeah, it'd just about take a King Arthur to fix this mess. This raw deal I got myself into.

I trudge down the sidewalk. I'm still hurting, but it's downhill all the way to Mom's and my apartment.

I slow and start scuffing my runners against the sidewalk. I'm dissatisfied. That picture I put together of what happened at Turpin's: it's bothering me again.

Why was Ray hiding in the back? That's the piece that doesn't fit.

But I don't have time to belabour the point. There's a *pop!* and a bullet whistles past my ear.

CHAPTER ELEVEN

I dive into a hedge. I smash through, emerging on the other side with leaves and twigs stuck to me. Then, sidestepping from the hole I've created, I squint through the leaves to the street.

A Mercedes flashes in front of me, its shiny green catching the soft rays of the early morning sun.

The car from the Manetas's driveway. Ray has followed me. She's decided that I know too much. I remember her threat: *You'll be toast.*

Obviously, a girl of her word.

I look at the house behind me. A kid in PJs is staring over a windowsill. He's sucking thoughtfully on his thumb. When he removes it, his first words could be: *Mommy, come see the stranger in our yard!*

I hope Mommy does. I hope Mommy phones the police.

Then, beyond the hedge — an engine purrs. Through the leaves I glimpse the Mercedes's polished green flanks. Ray's backing the car up, watching for me.

I don't have time to wait for good-citizen phone calls. Ignoring the pain in my ankle, I sprint around the back of the monster house and across a patio.

Laurel bushes border the backyard. I push through the thick, oval leaves into a parking lot.

A church looms in front of me. Its steeple rises high, glistening in the sun.

I hear footsteps in the yard behind.

I run to the church's side door, yank on the knob. Locked.

Laurel leaves rustle behind me. She's almost here.

I duck around a corner. I see another door, up a wheelchair ramp. It's propped open with a rock. I hoist myself to the edge of the ramp and scramble over the railing.

...

I'm so winded that, once inside, I lean against the wall and heave deep, ragged breaths. I summon enough energy to kick aside the rock holding the door open. I pull the door shut, twist the lock.

I'm in a kitchen. Grabbing a glass from the side of the sink, I run water into it. I glug the water back.

Over the rim of the glass, I see on the wall, just past the sink: a phone.

Before I can punch in 911, I hear a woman's soothing voice on the line.

" … so sad, Mrs. O'Leary. Jonathan will be missed by the community. He was always so good about driving the church bus on St. Monica's annual picnic day."

I heave another big breath, to interrupt and say that I have to call the police.

But, from the other person on the line, there's an explosion of weeping.

Gently I replace the receiver. Maybe there's a public phone somewhere.

I exit down a hall. From overhead, notes thunder up and down the scale. An organist doing warm-ups — in preparation for this guy Jonathan's funeral service, maybe.

I pass a large room with tables lining the sides. Women are setting out platters of sandwiches, the dainty triangular kind with the crusts cut off. Also pitchers of lemonade — and lots of tissue boxes.

One of the women pauses in arranging the sandwiches. She grabs a tissue and blows her nose.

Another woman, wearing a black pantsuit with a minister's collar, steps over to put an arm around her. This woman is tall, with short, sandy-coloured hair. Her bangs stand up, like she pushes them back a lot. Which might make someone else look comical, but her face is too calm for that. Too serene.

I expect to hear *There, there*s, and that kind of stuff, but the tall woman tells the other one, "Let it all out, Renata. That's what I just told your sister-in-law. Don't hold it back."

It's the same soothing voice I heard on the phone.

And, there's a phone just beyond her. That must've been the one she was using, and now it's free. If I can get to it.

I head into the room just as the plump woman wails, "To think that this was going to be a thank-you lunch, Reverend. St. Monica's way of showing its appreciation for Jonathan. We even baked his favourite cake: chocolate, with triple strawberry frosting, topped off with toffee twirls."

Nice as the minister is, she can't help herself. At the description of the cake, her face flickers with distaste. Another day I'd find this funny.

Not that, with Ray toting a gun outside, I'm too sure I'll have another day.

I get a few glances, but everyone's too busy fixing things up to pay much attention. I reach for the phone as the minister soothes Jonathan's sister, "At least we can serve the cake in Jonathan's memory."

I've punched in 911. I'm starting to sweat. What if the police don't believe my story?

But they'll have to. They'll find the Hannah's guy. He'll remember Jace coming in Turpin's front door. Yeah, he will. He will. And that will prove there were two servers in the restaurant. That will back up my story.

"Police emergency," says a brisk dispatcher. Maybe the same one I heard earlier, until the trucker drowned her out with his revving engine.

"My name's Colin — "

A louder wail erupts from Renata. "My brother! Jonathan!"

Along with everyone else, I turn to look at Renata.

Clutching the minister's arm, she's gazing across the room at a huge, strawberry-frosted cake with toffee swirls on top.

No, not at the cake. At the silver-framed photo someone is carefully setting down beside it.

At the pudgy man inside the frame.

I almost don't clue in. I almost don't get it.

The man in the photo is wearing a suit and tie, not jeans and leather jacket. He's smiling, not bleary-eyed and annoyed. He's noticeably younger.

It's his sister's earlier comment that tips me off. Staring at the guy in the photo, at his features that are familiar and yet not, my brain rewinds to Renata's description of the cake:

We even baked his favorite cake: chocolate, with triple strawberry frosting ...

A guy who likes his food in triplicate.

Jonathan, the dead man, was the trucker.

CHAPTER TWELVE

" ... Jonathan was my one witness. My one chance."

I sit back in Reverend Beth Brickell's stuffed armchair. I rub the heels of my palms over my eyes till fireworks flash against the lids. Not the most productive of responses to my situation. But at the moment I'm clean out of options — my last one having bit the dust along with Jonathan O'Leary.

The kettle on the minister's side table reaches a boil and whistles. Reverend Brickell pours the water over a teabag in a mug. She adds heaping spoonfuls of sugar.

Outside, two police cars are parked, waiting. The Reverend phoned them, asking that they wait outside till we're ready to meet them. Maybe *asked* isn't the right word. Beth Brickell has the type of serene voice that you don't say no to.

Ray would've scrammed at the sight of the cops. She's probably back on Panorama Ridge, fuming and plotting her next move.

I bet those green eyes aren't mocking right now. I bet they're smouldering hard enough to light a cigar from.

...

In the church hall, when I realized who Jonathan was, I almost passed out. Reverend Brickell helped me into her office, firmly closing the door against the other, oh-so-curious women.

Reverend Brickell stirs the tea and sugar with soft clanks of a spoon. "Jonathan O'Leary died an hour and a half ago at Lions Gate Hospital," she says. "He had the sense to go there and check himself in, rather than try to make the last of his deliveries. But by then it was too late. The strain was too much for his heart. He had a coronary and died."

The minister sits in the chair next to me. She presses the hot mug into my hands.

I drink, wincing. The tea is sugar-laden enough to slice. But it steadies me, forces me to focus on what she's saying.

"It was Staph," Reverend Brickell says. Her calm blue eyes search mine. "You know what that is?"

I think of those rows of meat patties, lined up with military precision on the Turpin's grill. "Yeah, food poisoning from undercooked meat?"

The minister nods. "The press is covering Jace's murder. They don't know yet about Jonathan's death from food poisoning. At Mrs. O'Leary's request, the police are keeping it out of the news as long as they can. She told me that a short while ago, when she phoned from the hospital."

I remember the sobbing voice I overheard on the kitchen phone; the despair that laced through every word like a weed.

Jonathan definitely had a grumpy side. *I came by earlier and you weren't even open. I thought the place had closed down. I got places to be, deadlines to meet, ya know?* But he'd been loved. And now he was gone. The ultimate raw deal.

I say, "Now I get why Jonathan was in a hurry this morning. He wanted to get his deliveries over with because you guys were holding a lunch for him."

"Yes. Jonathan was one of our few parishioners licensed to drive a bus. No matter how long his shift had been, he never refused when we asked him to drive our kids somewhere. He was a gem. The lunch was to be in his honour. Well," the minister says sadly, "it will be in his honour, but not the way we'd thought."

I shake my head. "I don't get why Jonathan got so sick. At 3 a.m., the patties were slow-cooking on the grill, just the way the midnight shift had left them. I turned the grill up and cooked 'em just like Jace instructed. Everything's carefully planned and timed at Turpin's to avoid undercooking."

Reverend Brickell says, "No one could blame you for Jonathan's death. It's the quality of Sam Turpin's meat that will be under investigation. Poor Sam. He's lost his son. He may lose his business, too, once the media get hold of a spoiled-meat scandal."

Spoiled. I've heard that word earlier — where? Oh, right. The old lady, whining about her laundry. *I time the drying of my linens. I allow for the freshness of morning dew ... you've spoiled them.*

Reverend Brickell urges, "You need to tell the police what you've told me, about Jace, and about Jonathan."

Of all the stuff that's happened this morning, it's the thought of Jonathan that chokes me up. He'd cruised by Turpin's earlier, and assumed it was closed. If only he'd given up and gone somewhere else.

Wait a minute. Mental rewind.

Jonathan said, *I thought the place had closed down.*

The old lady's face swims into my mind again. *I time the drying of my linens.*

It hits me. The piece of the picture that doesn't fit.

And, the new one that does.

I sit up, almost sloshing the tea out of the mug. "Jonathan didn't think Turpin's was closed. He thought it was closed *down.*"

...

Reverend Brickell waits, watching me, letting me work it out.

Setting the mug down, I pace across to a small TV set on top of the Reverend's bookcase. I switch the TV on, punch in the CBC Newsworld channel.

Once cable news has a hot story, they roll their footage over and over. Ordinarily I find this mind-numbing. Now I'm grateful for it.

The same anchorwoman is on, and sure enough, the camera soon cuts to the grainy security-camera video.

There's Jace walking up to the camera again. But before he does, the video flickers — just like it did on the TV in the Yarrows' basement.

I'd thought the flicker was just the Yarrows' old TV, struggling to warm up.

I was wrong.

"Jace wasn't there," I say tersely. "Not at 3:21 a.m. Somebody filmed him at another time. They set up some kind of feed, streaming the fake film into the camera. That flicker you saw — that was the moment the feed came in over the real-time video. If old man Turpin was watching, he'd have thought what I did: that his TV was briefly on the blink."

Reverend Brickell joins me in front of the TV. She studies Jace's laughing face, which he's shoved right up into the camera.

She says slowly, "So the fake video would contradict your claim, that you took over Jace's shift."

Jace's grin is getting to me. I switch the TV off. "Yeah, a frame-by-frame frame up, you might say. He and Ray would get the ransom money;

me, the blame."

The Reverend says, "The police will have specialists who can examine the video. They'll see that it's a fake."

Not *if* it's a fake. *That* it's a fake. I manage a wobbly grin at her. "Thanks for believing in me, Reverend."

She pats me on the shoulder. "I hope you now believe that you're not alone in the world. That you don't have to take care of every single thing yourself."

"Aw, I dunno, Rev. That might ruin my macho self-image."

She laughs. "Now you sit down and relax. I'm going outside to tell the police you need to have a long talk with them."

...

From inside the laurel bushes, I watch Reverend Brickell conferring with several cops. She's right: I need a long talk with them.

Just not yet.

Right now there's nothing to connect Ray to the phony kidnapping plot, to Jace's murder. But I have an idea how to prove she's involved right up to her beautiful eyeballs.

The Reverend is right about another thing. I don't have to do everything on my own.

That's why I called Bex from her office. Bex is going to help me convict Ray.

Turning, I run around the neighbouring house, to Cap Road.

CHAPTER THIRTEEN

This early in the day, there aren't any other visitors to the Capilano Suspension Bridge. Over by the totem poles, a custodian is spearing candy wrappers off the ground. He's a big guy, and his uniform doesn't quite fit. Maybe that's why he's scowling.

Then it's not the custodian I see, but, in my mind, a pair of scornful green eyes. *Dream on, loser. It'll never work*, they seem to jeer.

I push those green eyes out of my thoughts. I'll be seeing them, live, soon enough. When I do, I'm going to stare right into them and demand to know the truth. The whole truth, and nothing but.

For now, though, it's Bex I'm meeting.

There's a crunch on the gravel path.

"Colin?" she calls hesitantly.

...

"Bex. Thanks for coming."

Bex walks right up to me, her solemn eyes fixed on my face. "I want to help you."

She pauses, curious because I'm grinning.

"Sorry. I was thinking of an old joke between

me and my mom," I explain. "When I was a kid and had to do something I didn't want to, like start at yet another new school, Mom would say, 'Go on, Wart. Pull the sword from the stone.' That's pretty much what I'm facing right now."

Bex nods, but I can tell she's being polite. She thinks I'm losing it. She could be right. That slam on the skull probably cost me a few thousand brain cells.

"So how can I help you?" she asks. "How can we nail Rachel Manetas?"

"We can't," I reply.

At Bex's puzzled expression, I take her elbow and steer her toward a couple of logs in front of a colourful, and kind of angry-looking, carved snake. We each sit on a log. The custodian glances at us. Maybe we're not supposed to sit here. But with a shrug, he walks away.

The park is very still. Two hundred thirty feet down, Cap River crashes against the sharp canyon rocks. Its swirling waters glisten and wink in the sunlight.

I consider how to explain what I've figured out. Bex waits, her large hazel eyes on my face. She doesn't start gabbing like a lot of girls would.

Go on, Wart. Pull the sword from the stone.

I say, "Have you ever taken a wrong turn? You didn't realize it, and you kept going?"

Bex frowns. She doesn't understand.

"That's what I did," I say. "I watched the security-tape video of Jace at Turpin's. I made the first of my mental wrong turns. I accepted the video as real.

"But Ray fed another film into the camera. That's why she was hiding in Turpin's. While she was substituting the fake film, she had to turn the power off. That's why there's a flicker at the start of the tape. And that's why the Hannah's trucker thought Turpin's had closed down — because, when he first drove by, that 24-hour red neon sign was off."

Bex just stares. She doesn't get what the trucker has to do with this. Jonathan hasn't made the news yet.

I tell her, "While Ray was working on the camera, the grill was off. The burgers weren't cooking. The meat I served the trucker was still partly raw — and he died from it."

Bex's freckles blaze against her suddenly white face. "No. No … "

"Yeah," I say bitterly. I sit back against the plank. "You told me you and the other kids who hang out in the school basement are called 'moles.' Moles live in darkness, right, Bex?"

She moves her lips to reply. She can't. They're too dry.

"I'm guessing you guys are into photography. I'm guessing you're called moles because you're always working in a darkroom."

Bex gets up. She still looks frightened, but her hazel eyes are thinning, razor-like. When I met her, I thought how beautiful her eyes were. They're not beautiful now. They're wary, calculating.

I stand up, too. I'm remembering the black-and-white landscapes in the Yarrows' TV room. Lonely, forlorn photos — beautiful, in a haunting kind of way.

I say, "I'm guessing you're a pro at every type of photography — including making videos and substituting them for live feeds."

...

Bex wipes her tongue over her lips. She croaks out, "But Rachel Manetas was Jace's accomplice. You said it yourself."

I nod. "That's where I made my second mental wrong turn. Jace told me he had a hot date with Rachel Manetas. Later, up on the old logging road, he said he was meeting 'Ray.' I assumed Ray was short for Rachel."

Bex darts her gaze around, as if looking for an escape route.

"The photos in your basement. They're yours, aren't they? They're really good, Bex. But it was the photo someone else took, of you and your mom, that riveted me. She seems to be crushing the oxygen out of you. The overbearing Flora Louise Yarrow."

Bex snaps, "Yeah, I think I know my mom's name."

She can't keep her gaze still. It keeps flittering.

It's catching. I glance around, too. The custodian's disappeared. There are still no other visitors to the bridge.

I wonder if that's what Bex is checking for. Other people.

But I don't pursue the thought. There's one last thing I have to get clear. I'm remembering the fiercely magic-markered capital letters on the DVD cases.

" 'Flora Louise Yarrow,' " I repeat. "The initials spell F-L-Y. Sometimes nicknames come from initials, would you agree?"

Bex's hazel gaze swings back to me. "Nobody ever called my mother 'Fly.' If they did, she'd wallop them, and good."

"Yeah," I agree wearily. "I'm sure she would. But your name. Bex. That has to be a nickname. Cute one. Short for ... Becky?"

Bex jams her hands inside her windbreaker pockets.

"Which is short for — let's see. *Rebecca*?"

Her knuckles show through the fabric as she clenches her fists.

I smile, not with a whole lot of good humour, at her. "So, Rebecca Yarrow. What's your middle name? Anne? Amy? Whatever. The point is that your middle name starts with an A, doesn't it? So that your initials spell out: R-A-Y."

CHAPTER FOURTEEN

Bex pulls her right hand from her jacket pocket. She's holding the gun.

She says, quite calmly, "You should have stuck to your original plan, Colin. You should've pinned it on Rachel Manetas. I would've backed you up, said I overheard Rachel and Jace planning the fake kidnapping. Whatever it took, I would have done it. I liked you."

She sounds genuinely regretful. I even see tears forming.

Maybe I can get through to her. "Talk to me," I say. I don't look at the gun. "Tell me about Jace."

The tears slide down her face, and she doesn't bother wiping them away. "Jace had the shift before me, early Saturdays. He was always nice when I showed up at six. Joked around, wished me a good day, and all that.

"Then, one morning, he noticed me. I mean, really noticed me. Me, one of the nobodies! It was like being lit up by a sunbeam."

Her face brightens now, remembering. I consider lunging for the gun. But any sudden act might scare Bex into firing.

"Jace said, 'You're one of the moles. What a waste for a girl like you to hide in that basement darkroom all the time. Come out with me and have some fun.' So," Bex smiles dreamily, "we started seeing each other. We kept it secret, avoided the usual hangouts. Jace even invented his own, private nickname for me, 'Ray.' A love name, he called it. That way, if I phoned his house, his dad wouldn't know who I was. Jace said Mr. Turpin wouldn't approve of our relationship, what with me being, well … not in their circle."

I wonder about that. I bet Jace kept the lid on Bex because he was hatching his phony-kidnap plan even then.

As if tapping into my thoughts, Bex says, "Jace thought up this scheme to get dough out of his dad. Then we wouldn't have to care what the old man thought. We could go off somewhere."

I wonder about that, too. I'm guessing Jace was just sweet-talking Bex, to win her cooperation. But still I don't interrupt.

"Jace said all we needed was to find someone who looked sort of like him. Some patsy who'd think, yeah, all Jace wants is a fill-in for the early Saturday shift."

Also some patsy who was lonely, I think. Like me. Like Bex. Jace preyed on the loners. He knew they were the most vulnerable.

Bex's glance drifts over the bridge, to the swirling river far below. She doesn't see it, though. She's still dreamy-eyed about Jace. The girl is in la-la love land.

My chance to rush her, grab the gun, is now.

But I've misjudged Bex. I barely move — and *crack!* She jerks back the safety catch. Her hazel eyes stare at me down the length of the gun.

"And now," Bex says, still in that dreamy, soft voice, "I have to kill you. Just like I killed Jace when I met up with him on the old logging road."

...

Gun pointed at my heart, Bex is waving me down the slope to the suspension bridge.

"I'm going to give you a chance, Colin. I won't shoot you — you can jump."

I look down to the swirling green river, laced with angry white foam and punctured with jagged rocks.

Some chance. And Bex can pretend my jump was an accident.

Jace underestimated his shy little mole.

"Wait a minute," I say. "Why did you have to kill Jace?"

I can guess the answer — it has green eyes and slinky moves — but I'm playing for time.

Bex waves the gun at me in a gesture to start walking. I take backward steps, so I have a pretext for going slow.

The first visitors of the day filter into the park. Without a glance at us, they place a cooler on a picnic table and sit down.

Bex positions herself with her back to them. "Keep moving."

I backstep some more. Something jabs me in the back: the start of the bridge's metal rail.

Bex motions me onward. Holding the rail, I backstep down the swaying bridge.

She follows, keeping the beady eye of the gun's barrel trained on me.

...

"Everything was fine with Jace, all through the summer," Bex explains. "And then school started, and Rachel showed up. Jace's gaze was duct-taped to her. And Rachel was sly. She pretended she wasn't interested in Jace. Like anyone could not be.

"So, I confronted Jace. He admitted it." Fresh tears spring to Bex's eyes. The girl has more water in her than Cap River.

"Jace said we should stay away from each other, anyway, what with the fake kidnap coming up. He'd split the ransom with me, and that would be that."

I scan the park for the custodian. No sign of him. Just the picnickers at the table. The park is quiet, eerily so. Is it just me, or does Bex notice that, too?

"Know what?" Bex whines. "Jace was smiling while he dumped me. As if that made it all right. Well, it didn't. No one messes with Rebecca Yarrow."

Bex's freckled face lumps into a deep scowl. For that instant she morphs into her mom. I bet soppy-DVD-fan Mrs. Yarrow cries a lot, too. Mom and daughter are sentimental — and hard as those rocks waiting to receive me below.

I recall Bex's sweet, urgent face in the basement when the sirens were shrilling. She'd pressed the BLT sandwich on me — because she was trying to delay me, to get me caught.

Bex is saying, "Rachel agreed to go out with Jace last night. The same night we were going to pull off the fake kidnap! I told him he was nuts. He laughed; said it'd be good cover. He'd get Rachel drunk, and she wouldn't remember when the date ended. She'd be his alibi."

I look straight at Bex. "And who will be your alibi for right now, Bex?"

There's a sweetness about her confused look. Yeah, she's sweet all right — sweet poison. "I don't need an alibi, Colin. I'll say you confessed to kidnapping and killing Jace. You were scared, so you committed suicide."

I say, "I stopped Jace's Mustang at the side of the road. A car zoomed past me. I'm betting that was you, heading back after you'd shot Jace. You wanted to be sure to make your shift on time. To slip back into sweet, normal, everyday Bex mode."

I step sideways to glance down at Cap River. The bridge sways. My guts twist.

Bex steps sideways, too. In her white-knuckle grip, the gun follows me like a homing device.

"You're going to jump," she says. "If you don't, I'll shoot you."

She can't mean it, not with those picnickers back there, in the park. She can't take the chance they'll look up. She's bluffing. She has to be.

I think of that rushing current, those sharp, pointy rocks.

"Forget it," I tell her.

Bex shrugs, and fires.

CHAPTER FIFTEEN

The sound of the shot whistles around the canyon.

Bex gapes at the hole in my jacket. She squints through it to the damaged, but not punctured, vest behind.

The bullet-proof vest, to be exact. The vest the police outfitted me with at St. Monica's, along with a wire. Just before I made a big show of sneaking out, in case Bex was watching.

Because I've learned that Reverend Brickell is right. I don't have to deal with everything on my own, all the time.

I talked to the police — not the long talk I'll have with them later, but enough to formulate a plan with them.

A plan to catch Bex.

I take advantage of Bex's stunned expression to tackle her to the floor of the bridge. I twist the gun out of her hand and spin it along the bridge behind me. I'd like to throw it over the rail, but I know the cops want it for evidence.

Bex claws, scratches and kicks. This is where the vest is a drawback. I'm bigger than Bex, but the vest is heavy, weighing me down.

The more we struggle, the wider the bridge swings. It's bending sideways. Screaming, Bex lets go of me and grips the chain-link sides of the bridge. I crawl to grab the gun before it slides off, down to the rushing waters below.

The bridge spins up into its steepest arc yet. The movement rolls me on to the chain links. The gun's grey metal gleams, not a foot away. I grab it —

Just as Bex, hanging from the chain links on the opposite side, slams me hard with her feet.

With my free hand, I flail at the links, trying to find a hold. *Wham!* Her feet deck me again.

Then —

Cops pound on to the bridge from both ends. With their weight on its floor, the bridge suddenly settles.

A hand yanks Bex off me.

With his other hand, the custodian helps me up. "It's all right, son. I gotcha."

Bex is still kicking, but a woman — one of the picnickers — runs up behind and grabs her.

...

Several cops wearing black, SWAT-labelled jackets carry rifles. This was part of my deal with the North Van Police Department. If Bex aimed the gun at my head instead of my vest-protected chest, a SWATster would shoot it out of her hand.

"But she didn't," Detective Herfst says. He looks a lot cheerier than when he was pretending to be a custodian, spiking bits of garbage. "And not because she was anxious to spare your natural good looks. Hostage-takers instinctively position their guns in front of their chests, so anybody around has less chance of noticing."

Detective Herfst sits me down at the picnic table. Closer up, I see the cooler is set on its side. It contains not food, but a transmission unit the "picnickers" were using to receive Bex's and my conversation.

Another cop takes my jacket as evidence, for the bullet hole. Herfst helps me out of the vest, whose strong metal fibers trapped the bullet. He carefully untapes the wire from my chest.

Helicopters bearing the logos of TV and radio stations buzz overhead. The gusts from the propellers bend the peaks of the fir trees.

Herfst brings me a SWAT jacket to wear. Glancing up at the 'copters, he shrugs. "As long as you were facing down Bex — Rebecca Anne Yarrow, that is — we sealed off the park and kept the airspace clear. Now the media are swarming. For the next few days, everywhere you look around Cap Canyon, you'll see the natural beauty of a thousand microphones."

I nod. "I was worried Bex would wonder why such a popular attraction was almost empty. On a sunny Saturday, too. But I guess Bex couldn't think of everything."

"They never do," Detective Herfst says confidently.

...

I wish I had some of his confidence a little while later, when Rachel Manetas walks toward me.

I stand and grunt a hello. Then I loaf awkwardly, unable to think of anything to say. *Sorry I suspected you of murder* seems kind of lame.

Rachel doesn't bother with niceties. "The police let me through because they need a statement from me," she says. "It's my mom's Mercedes that Bex stole. When I saw the car was missing, I checked my purse. The keys were gone."

I remember the purse lying sideways outside the terrace doors. "Bex knew I'd come to talk to you. I guess she eavesdropped, and lifted the keys." At Rachel's unfriendly gaze, I shrug. "You just can't trust anyone these days."

That produces a scowl. "I don't know how you can joke, Colin Wirt."

"I don't know, either."

Rachel looks around at the tall firs being grazed by 'copter blades. She blurts, "I admitted to the police that I was out with Jace last night. I want to tell you about it, too. I don't know why I feel I owe it to you, since all you've done is upset me."

I start to apologize, but she holds up her hand. "Jace had been after me to go out with him for weeks. Finally, this week, he told me his family had a pass for night skiing at Grouse. He and his parents were going Friday night, and I could join them.

"I thought, okay, if the parents are along, it's not really a date, right? And I've always wanted to go night skiing.

"Well, Jace picks me up at nine, and we go for a burger at Turpin's." She rolls her eyes. "I get the two-hour Biography-channel treatment on Jace's life. What a great guy he is, what a jock. Then we head up to Grouse. Except, the mountain's shut down. There's no night skiing, and no sign of his parents.

"We just sit there, in Jace's car, at the base of the mountain. Jace produces a bottle of scotch. I tell him I just want to go home. But Jace gets ugly." Rachel hesitates, trying to compose herself. "So, I grab the bottle and slam it over his head."

I stretch out a hand and clasp one of hers. She pulls away. "Blood starts flowing from Jace's right temple. I jump out of the car and run all the way home. I'm scared he's going to follow me. Scared he'll press charges. I don't sleep all night — and then you show up early in the morning, accusing me of killing Jace."

"Oh, man." I sit back. "Well, that explains the skis in Jace's trunk."

At her puzzled expression, I explain, "Jace and Bex bashed me in the skull, then locked me in the trunk. It's a long, lurid story. You don't want to hear it. Not right now, not after what you've been through."

Rachel catches the tiredness in my voice. Her scowl fades. She says slowly, "I thought I'd been through a lot. But I didn't know what had happened to you. Geez, Colin."

I spread out my hands. "I'm burned out, Rachel. That's why I keep making dumb jokes. That's about all I'm capable of. I actually have a lot I'd like to say to you. Starting with the fact that, even when I thought you were a murderer, I liked you. Beat up and bitter as I was, all I could think was how totally much I liked you."

"Really." She's not smiling, but there's the faintest glimmer in those so-green eyes.

Detective Herfst is heading toward us. "Okay, guys. Let's go to the station and talk."

He gestures to a cop car by the ticket booth. We walk with him to the car.

"So," Rachel murmurs to me. "What's with the SWAT jacket, Colin?"

"I dunno. I thought I might get into the fly-disposal business."

"You're right. The jokes are dumb."

But, at last, she's smiling.

THE END

ABOUT THE AUTHOR

Scottish-born and mystery-minded, Melanie Jackson is an award-winning children's/young adult author and former journalist. A volunteer creative-writing mentor with the Vancouver School Board, Melanie is also on the board of directors of the BC branch of the International Reading Association. Her previous novel with Midway Press is No Way Out (2010). Melanie lives with her family in Vancouver.

Melanie thanks the Midway team for great assistance in the production of this book: publisher Louise Wallace, editor Harry Goldhar, cover designer Otto Pfannschmidt, and the infinitely patient layout artist/copy editor Violet Pilkey.